BLUE MONDAY AND FRIDAY THE THIRTEENTH

SUNDAY MONDAY TUESDAY

WEDNESDAY THURSDAY FRIDAY

SATURDAY SUNDAY MONDAY

TUESDAY WEDNESDAY THURSDAY

BLUE MONDAY
AND FRIDAY
THE THIRTEENTH

by Lila Perl

illustrated by Erika Weihs

CLARION BOOKS

TICKNOR & FIELDS: A HOUGHTON MIFFLIN COMPANY

New York

Sec 711
chap 53
Law of 1985

To Ann Troy,
for whose enthusiasm,
insight, and encouragement
I am ever grateful

The author gratefully acknowledges permission to quote the first stanza of "Thursday" by Edna St. Vincent Millay. From *Collected Poems*, Harper & Row. Copyright 1922, 1950 by Edna St. Vincent Millay.

Clarion Books
Ticknor & Fields, a Houghton Mifflin Company
Text copyright © 1986 by Lila Perl
Illustrations copyright © 1986 by Erika Weihs
Printed in the U.S.A.

Library of Congress Cataloging in Publication Data
Perl, Lila.
Blue Monday and Friday the Thirteenth.
Bibliography: p.
Includes index.
Summary: Focuses on each day of the week, describing the cultural and linguistic origin of the name, the popular superstitions connected with that day, and the major holidays falling on that day.
1. Days — Juvenile literature. [1. Days]
I. Weihs, Erika, ill. II. Title.
GR930.P47 1986 398'.33 85-13051
ISBN 0-89919-327-7

Q 10 9 8 7 6 5 4 3 2 1

Contents

The seven-day week probably started in ancient times in Babylonia

The Week

A day, a week, a month, a year — these measurements of time are very familiar to us. We accept them almost without thinking. We say that a day has twenty-four hours, a week has seven days, and so forth.

Some of the time divisions on our calendar are based on careful scientific observation of the moon, the sun, and the other stars. But not all. For example, there is no scientific reason why a week should have seven days.

Among some ancient peoples, a week was as short as four days; among others it was as long as nine or even thirteen days. As recently as two hundred years ago, during the period of the French Revolution, France had a calendar with a ten-day week. And there are peoples in the world today whose weeks are shorter or longer than seven days.

The word *week* doesn't even mean "seven." It is probably

The phases of the moon as it completes its cycle in roughly twenty-nine and a half days

related to the German word *Wechsel*, which simply means "change." Everybody needs a change, a way of dividing up the succession of days into meaningful units of time. Long before our present-day calendar existed, different groups of people made up their own divisions.

Some divisions were based on market days. If a market was held every fourth, or fifth, or eighth day, then that was when the week began, or perhaps ended.

Other divisions may have been based on the phases of the moon. The seven-day week probably began 4,000 to 5,000 years ago among the people of Babylonia, in western Asia.

It takes about twenty-nine and a half days for the moon to grow from a new moon to a crescent moon, a half moon, a full moon, and then back again to a thin, waning crescent. These moon changes were very easy to follow. The ancient Babylonians must have decided to divide the moon's cycle into groups of days, and they chose the number seven. Perhaps they did this because seven was a whole number that fit fairly well into twenty-nine and a half. Of course, their plan was not perfect because a seven-day week multiplied by four comes to only twenty-eight days.

There may have been another reason why the Babylonians decided there should be seven days in their week. Like other early peoples, they observed that there were seven clearly seen heavenly bodies. They were the sun, the moon, and five of the planets. The Romans later named those planets Mercury, Venus, Mars, Jupiter, and Saturn, after the gods they worshipped.

Today, of course, we have evidence of nine planets, one of which is Earth. Uranus, Neptune, and Pluto, the three most distant planets, were too faint to be seen without a telescope. Perhaps, if the Babylonians *had* been able to see those three, our week would now consist of ten days instead of seven. What a long stretch there would be from Sunday to Sunday!

In any case, the seven heavenly bodies seemed to have magical properties to the Babylonians. So, for them, seven became not only the number of days in the week but also a sacred as well as a lucky number.

Naturally, in an era when communications were extremely limited, it took a very long time for the idea of a seven-day week to get around. The ancient Egyptians had also observed the phases of the moon. To them it seemed that ten was the number that fit best into the twenty-nine and a half day cycle. So they divided their month into three ten-day weeks. The word *month* comes, of course, from *moon*.

The Chinese, another ancient civilization, developed a

calendar with a cycle of sixty days, each having a different name. But because the cycle was so long, it too was broken up into ten-day weeks.

In the Americas, the Aztec and Mayan Indians of what are now Mexico and Guatemala had twenty different day names. But their weeks were thirteen days long. This meant that all the names of the days did not get used up in one week. Some were left over for the following week. Although this system sounds confusing, the calendars of these early Indian peoples were very well thought out and highly accurate.

The Indians of the more northerly parts of America used a simpler system. Time was reckoned chiefly by the moon's cycle. Some groups counted twelve moons to a year and some counted thirteen. A trip of some distance might take one or two moons. Three, four, or five moons might pass between the time of planting corn or squash or tobacco and the time of harvesting.

The northern Indian peoples appear not to have had any names for the days or to have divided the moon's cycle into weeks. To keep track of the days of the month, they would simply pile up twenty-nine or thirty sticks. Each day, beginning with the first appearance of the growing, or waxing, moon, they would remove one stick from the heap. When none were left, a month had passed and a new one was ready to begin.

Even the ancient Romans, with their great military, engineering, and other skills of organization, never thought to give names to the days. Instead, they divided each month somewhere near its middle and called the thirteenth or the fifteenth day "the ides." (The ides never fell on the fourteenth day because the Romans believed even numbers were unlucky.)

The first day of the Roman month was called "the calends." The word *calends* comes from the Latin meaning "to proclaim." Also, this word has given us the word *calendar*.

Keeping track of time by removing one stick a day from a numbered pile

There were so many days between the calends and the ides that the Romans also gave a name to the ninth day before the ides. They called it "the nones." In counting backward from the ides to the nones, they included the ides. So, if the ides fell on the fifteenth of *Martius* (March), for example, the nones would be on the seventh. In shorter months, like *Aprilis* (April), the ides were on the thirteenth and the nones were on the fifth.

The custom of counting backward made this clumsy system even more awkward. The Romans spoke of "the third day before the nones," "the second day before the ides," "the eighth day before the calends" (really the previous month). In Shakespeare's play *Julius Caesar*, the Roman general and statesman is warned by a soothsayer to "Beware the ides of March." And, indeed, Caesar was stabbed to death in the Roman senate on March 15 in the year 44 B.C. Imagine how unpoetic the soothsayer's words would have been if he had had to warn Caesar to beware of the "twelfth day before the calends," or of some other ungainly date.

If there was such a thing as a week on the Roman calendar, it was the period between market days. Markets were held every ninth day. But they were probably most meaningful to the people who lived in the countryside and who gathered to sell their farm products. The citizens of the city of Rome itself had many special days set aside each month for games and other public events.

The Jews of the ancient world were almost certainly responsible for spreading the idea of the seven-day week. As they too had lived in western Asia, they adopted it in quite early times. They are believed to have introduced the seven-day week to Egypt when they journeyed to that land over 3,000 years ago. As a result, the Egyptians abandoned their ten-day week.

The strongest influence leading to the adoption of the seven-day week came from the Hebrew Bible, which is called the Old Testament. This earliest portion of the Bible was written by the Jews. It was probably begun about 750 years before the birth of Christ. In the Book of Genesis, we are told that God made the world in six days and rested on the seventh day. That day became the Jewish Sabbath, or weekly holy day.

The early Christians, as well as the Romans and Greeks among whom they were living, chose the seven-day week. With the growth of Christianity, the week of seven days began to be even better known and more widely accepted.

Now, too, certain peoples began to give names to each of the seven days. The Romans named the days mainly for the sun, the moon, and some of their gods and goddesses. The northern Europeans did the same. But of course their language was different from the Latin of the Romans, and their gods had different names. Most of the day-names that have come to us in English are Scandinavian in origin.

Other peoples, however, have never given names to most of the days of the week. The Hebrew word for Sunday, as in the Old Testament, means "first day"; Monday is "second day"; and so forth. Only the seventh day, the Sabbath, is called by a name: *Shabbat*.

There are Christian peoples, too, who indicate the days by numbers rather than names. In Portuguese, Greek, Hungarian, Serbo-Croatian, and other tongues, only Sunday, the Christian Sabbath, and Saturday, may have special names.

Moslems also call most of their days by numbers. The Arabic name for Friday, however, is "day of gathering." This is because Friday is the Moslem holy day.

For well over a thousand years, the seven-day week remained the standard in countries that had been influenced by the biblical telling of the creation of the world. Then, in the late 1700s, a sudden change took place in one country of Europe. The makers of the French Revolution decided to work out a calendar of their own. It was their way of saying, "Down with the past; down with all the old traditions!"

The new French calendar started on the day the monarchy was abolished and a republic was declared. France would no longer be ruled by a king. The date was September 22, 1792, In France, that day became the first day of the year I.

Many other changes took place. All the months were renamed and given thirty days each. However, twelve times thirty comes to only 360 days. A year needs to have 365 days, for that is approximately the length of time it takes for the Earth to make one complete revolution around the sun. So the French calendar-makers added five days to the end of their year. When a leap year came along, every fourth year, they tacked on a sixth day.

Now that all the months had thirty days, the French decided there should be three ten-day weeks in each month. The week was known as a *décade*. The days lost their names and were called by number starting with *primidi* (first day), *duodi* (second day), *tridi* (third day), and so on all the way to *décadi* (tenth day). The week was, of course, terribly long. So *décadi* was designated a day of rest.

The old Roman-based names for the months, like January,

February, March, and so forth, were done away with. The French thought it a good idea to name their months after the seasons. So, as their calendar began in September, they named the first month Vendémiaire, after "vintage," or wine-making time. The last month was called Fructidor for the late-summer ripening of fruits.

Although the French Revolutionary calendar appeared very neat, logical, and even poetic in many ways, it was a disaster. The seasonally named months might be suitable for France, but they were all wrong for other climates. To carry on relations abroad, the young republic had to translate all its dates, including month, day, and year.

Yet the calendar continued in effect for a little over thirteen years. It was not until the close of 1805, a short time into the Revolutionary year XIV, that the French at last abandoned it. They went back to the old calendar, including the seven-day week.

Today most of us can't imagine what it would be like to have a week that was longer or shorter than seven days. The rhythm of the days is deeply implanted in us. We notice this when our week is reshaped by a holiday that falls on a weekday, when we are on vacation, or when other changes take place that upset our daily routine.

There's no question that Sunday "feels" different from Tuesday, that Friday generally gives us a great sense of relief that the school or work week is just about over.

What events have taken place in the past to give the days of the week their special characters? Why do they have certain associations for us? How did they get their names? What are their stories?

A Puritan family dressed for church on Sunday

All About Sunday

How then was the Devil dressed?
O, he was in his Sunday's best;
His coat was red, and his breeches were blue,
And there was a hole where his tail came through.
                    Robert Southey: *The Devil's Walk*

Of all the days that's in the week
I dearly love but one day,
And that's the day that comes betwixt
A Saturday and Monday.
                    Henry Carey: *Sally in Our Alley*

Sunday may or may not be your favorite day. It's nice to think of having one whole day in which to be lazy. It's pleasant to be able to follow your fancy or do things that are different from what you do the rest of the week.

Of course, this doesn't mean that Sunday has no rules at all. In many parts of the world Sunday used to mean — and still means — getting dressed in your best clothes, going to church or Sunday school, visiting relatives, and sitting down to a big family dinner.

On the other hand, Sundays aren't as formal as they used to be. Many of the rules of behavior for that day have been relaxed. In fact, more people go to work on Sundays than ever before. One reason is that nowadays stores often remain open for Sunday shoppers, not only just before Christmas but all year round. Sunday is also a popular day for sporting events, as well as other forms of entertainment and recreation. Movies, museums, restaurants, and even theater performances draw Sunday crowds.

Although Sunday is the Sabbath, or weekly holy day, for almost all the world's Christians, its name goes back to long before the birth of Christianity. Among the heavenly bodies that entranced and baffled the ancients, surely the most important was the sun.

The Egyptians worshipped a sun god whom they called Ra. They knew that without the light and warmth of the sun, there would be no crops. If Ra failed them, their great civilization would die. The god Ra was painted and carved on the tomb walls and in the temples of ancient Egypt. Sometimes he was shown as a male figure having the head of a falcon and crowned with a great sun-disk standing on its rim.

One Egyptian pharaoh, or king, abandoned all of Egypt's other gods. He chose to worship the sun only. In his religion, the sun was depicted as a huge disk in the sky casting its rays upon the earth. Each ray ended in a kindly hand curved into a gesture of blessing.

Where, though, did the sun go at night? This was a great mystery to all early peoples. They did not know that the Earth was round and that it spun on its axis around the sun. They had no idea that when it was dark in their part of the world, the sun was shining in some other part.

They only knew that for them the sun sank in the west

The Egyptian god of the sun, Ra

each evening and disappeared. To the Egyptians, the desert that lay on the western bank of the Nile River was the land of the dying sun. So it was there that they built the great pyramids and other tombs for their kings, queens, and nobles. The burial sites across the river were called "cities of the dead."

People who lived by the sea had their own legends regarding the setting of the sun. Many thought that the great ball of fire sizzled each evening as it dipped down into the chilly distant waters.

The ancient Greeks believed they had an answer to the rising, setting, and rising again of the sun. Their sun god was called Helios. He was said to wear a golden helmet and to drive across the sky in a golden chariot pulled by four white horses. Each day his chariot soared in a flaming arc from east to west. At night, he silently sailed his chariot and horses back to the east on a golden ship. In the morning, he was ready to start his skyward journey to the west again.

While Helios embodied the sun itself, another Greek god, Apollo, expressed the beauty and goodness of the sun. Apollo was the god of light, of healing, and also of music, poetry, and prophecy.

The ancient Romans borrowed many of the gods of Greece, including Apollo. They, too, were dazzled by the forces of nature and especially by the sun. So, when they adopted the seven-day week, it isn't surprising that they named the first day *dies solis,* or day of the sun. After all, in the Old Testament it was written that on the first day God said: "Let there be light."

Yet, the word *Sunday* doesn't really come to us directly

from the Latin of the ancient Romans. It comes by way of ancient German and Scandinavian peoples who also followed the worship of the sun.

Between five and six hundred years after the birth of Christ, some of these peoples, known as Angles and Saxons, invaded the British Isles. They came from the area that is today southern Denmark and northern Germany. The Anglo-Saxon, or Old English, word for the day of the sun was *sunnandaeg*. It's easy to see how this word became *Sunday* in modern English.

The word for Sunday in other present-day languages of northern Europe shows the close relationship of those tongues to English. Here are some examples:

German — Sonntag
Dutch — Zondag
Danish — søndag
Norwegian — søndag
Swedish — söndag

During the time that these words for Sunday were starting to develop to the north, a change had taken place in the Roman world. The early Christians who lived in the far-flung Roman Empire began to call *dies solis* by a new name: *dies dominicus*, or day of the Lord.

They did so because it was on that day of the week that Jesus Christ was believed to have risen from the dead. His resurrection, as this miracle was called, took place two days after he had died on the cross. Nowadays, the day of Christ's death is known as Good Friday and the day of his resurrection as Easter Sunday.

For the early Christians, however, Sunday remained a workday. People worshipped privately. It was not until about three hundred years after the death of Christ that both the church and the state officially recognized Sunday as the Christian Sabbath. Today, there are only a few Christian sects, such as the Seventh-Day Adventists, that observe Saturday, the Sabbath of the Old Testament, as their weekly holy day.

The change from *dies solis* to *dies dominicus* had some far-reaching effects. It explains why modern languages that come from Latin have words for Sunday that are very different from English. All of them, of course, mean Lord's day or God's day rather than sun day:

French — dimanche
Italian — domenica
Spanish — domingo
Portuguese — domingo
Romanian — duminică

In the United States, Sunday began as a very strict day of worship. Starting in the 1600s, several New England colonies enforced rigid rules of behavior to make sure that the Lord's day was properly observed.

The Puritans of Massachusetts, for example, were required to spend six hours or more at the religious meetinghouse, praying, reading from the Bible, and listening to sermons. Even young children had to attend. They were watched over by a church official with a big stick in case any mischief broke out. Newborns were brought to be baptized in the unheated meetinghouses of New England in weather so cold that the water in the baptismal basin froze.

The New England tradition of eating baked beans on Saturday night was related to the demands of the Sunday Sabbath. The housewife had to spend all day Saturday readying her household and her family for Sunday. So the easiest dish to prepare on Saturday was a pot of beans, flavored with salt pork and molasses, that could simmer all day in the fireplace oven.

On Sunday itself no cooking or housework — not even making beds or sweeping — was permitted. Shaving, haircutting, kissing, running, whistling, or traveling anywhere but to the meetinghouse was forbidden. Even being born on a Sunday was considered something of a sin, and sometimes the unlucky parents were forced to pay a fine.

The Puritans of New Haven Colony in Connecticut put these and other rules into printed form and bound them in blue paper. As a result, they came to be known as "blue laws."

The laws spelled out penalties as severe as whipping, banishment, and imprisonment for a number of crimes. Not all had to do with breaking the Sabbath. Some were general prohibitions against dancing, card playing, playing musical instruments, and even baking mince pies. The last is probably explained by the fact that the Puritans were also forbidden to celebrate Christmas.

The Puritans were soon outnumbered by other colonists and immigrant groups with less strict views. Yet even today we can see the influence of the Puritan forefathers. There are still Sunday blue laws that require public institutions, shops, and other businesses to remain closed, that prohibit certain forms of entertainment, and that generally try to regulate public and private life on the Christian Sabbath.

Sunday school classes are held, of course, because they are connected with church-going. Usually they take place before or after services and offer Bible study and religious instruction for children in various age groups.

The first Sunday schools, however, were set up for a slightly different purpose. They are believed to have been started in England in the late 1700s for children who were employed in factories. The child laborers worked six days a week and had no chance to learn to read and write.

To teach reading, the schools used the Bible and other religious texts, and so they also taught religion. Classes lasted almost all day on Sunday. The sponsors of the Sunday schools boasted with pride of keeping the little factory workers off the streets and out of mischief on their day off. No one seemed to think that time for play was of any importance.

Nowadays the Sunday calendar in the United States is busier than ever. In addition to the old religious holidays that fall on Sunday, there are newer family holidays like Mother's Day and Father's Day. Sunday is also a popular day for parades and other festivals. New York City, for example, holds its Puerto Rican Day and other celebrations honoring its varied population groups on a Sunday.

Sunday, in fact, is so widely regarded as a holiday that when *another* holiday such as the Fourth of July or Christmas falls on a Sunday, we get Monday as an extra day to celebrate.

Here is a list of some special days that *always* fall on a Sunday, telling how they began and on which Sunday of the year they will occur:

Palm Sunday takes place in March or April, one week before Easter Sunday. In ancient times it was the custom in Eastern

Carrying palm leaves home from church on Palm Sunday

countries to carry palm branches in victory processions. Palm leaves were also strewn in the paths of famous persons to honor them.

According to the New Testament of the Bible, Jesus was honored in this way on the Sunday when he rode into the city of Jerusalem. He was loved by the people. Yet his death, carried out by the Roman rulers of Jerusalem, took place on the Friday of that week. So, for Christians, Palm Sunday became the first day of a solemn week known as Holy Week.

Palm Sunday observances probably first began in about the year 300. Some Christian churches have a procession and a Mass. Others have a simple service. Palm leaves are blessed in memory of those offered to Jesus. They may be taken home and kept. Some people make small crosses out of palm in remembrance of the death of Christ on the cross. In places where palms are not available, branches of olive, willow, or other trees may be blessed on Palm Sunday.

Easter Sunday is, of course, the day that Christ is believed to have risen from the dead. Miraculously, the tomb in which he had been buried was found to be empty. The early Christians did not have a fixed annual date for commemorating Christ's resurrection. So, in 325, a church council met to try to determine one. It decided that Easter Sunday should fall on the first Sunday, after the first full moon, on or after March 21.

As a result, Easter Sunday can occur as early as March 22 or as late as April 25. This holiday is known as a movable feast. So we must check the calendar each year for the first full moon of spring, counting spring from March 21. The word *Easter* itself comes from the Anglo-Saxon name for the goddess of spring, Eastre.

As if finding the right Sunday for Easter weren't confusing enough, there are really two Easters celebrated every year. Christians who are members of Eastern Orthodox churches observe Easter Sunday on a different date because an earlier, slightly erroneous calendar is used for calculation. Most Greeks and many other eastern Europeans, as well as Egyptian and Asian Christians, belong to the Eastern church.

The celebration of Easter Sunday really begins with the last strokes of midnight, as the new day is ushered in. Some churches hold midnight vigils with processions and the lighting of candles. Others have sunrise services or regular morning services. At the close of the Easter Sunday service, people may greet each other with the words: "Christ is risen."

Easter is closely bound up with the season of spring, and both are connected with rebirth and new life. So it isn't surprising that eggs, fresh spring flowers, baby animals such as rabbits, chicks, and lambs, and even new clothes are among the popular Easter symbols.

Mother's Day takes place on the second Sunday in May. In the United States, the idea of setting aside a special day for honoring mothers began in the late 1800s. Local churches, women's groups, and peace organizations held ceremonies at various times in the spring.

In 1914, Mother's Day became a national observance with a specific day designated. An early Mother's Day custom was to wear a carnation in one's buttonhole — pink or red if one's mother was alive; white if she was dead.

Nowadays Mother's Day has become very commercial. Florists, department stores, gift shops, candy and greeting-card manufacturers, and restaurants do a thriving business. The idea of remembering one's mother on a given day is no doubt a good one. Numerous countries around the world have a similar celebration. Best of all, of course, is to direct kind thoughts and acts toward one's loved ones throughout the year.

Father's Day takes place on the third Sunday in June. It naturally followed that, if mothers were to be honored with a special day, fathers should be too. It was first recommended that Father's Day should be observed nationally in 1924. It, too, has been very good for business, as it is a major gift-giving holiday.

The success of Mother's Day and Father's Day has spurred the appointing of special days for other family members. Some examples are *Grandparents' Day* (the first Sunday after the first Monday in September) and *Mother-in-Law's Day* (the fourth Sunday in October). However, neither seems to have caught on very strongly yet. Perhaps the public sees these attempts to expand the list as going a bit too far.

Finally, Sunday is the day of the week on which daylight saving time in the United States goes into effect each year. At 2 A.M. on the last Sunday in April we set our clocks ahead one hour to convert from standard time to daylight time. Then, at 2 A.M. on the last Sunday in October, we set our clocks back one hour and return to standard time.

Daylight saving delays the coming of darkness by one hour. It began during World War I as a temporary economy measure to cut down on the use of fuel for electricity. It was used again during World War II and, in some parts of the country, afterward.

Of course, pushing the clock forward means that it begins to grow light an hour later in the morning. For years, farmers and others who had to start work very early opposed daylight saving. People who began their work day later seemed to like the idea of having an extra hour of daylight in the evening. So some communities went on daylight time and others didn't.

This created terrible confusion in transportation schedules, phone service, and other communications. At last, in 1967, the Uniform Time Act went into effect. The entire country was to go on daylight time from April to October. An individual state, however, could remain on standard time provided the entire state agreed to do so by law.

Since Sunday is still the day that the fewest people have to go to work or school, it is probably the best day for getting accustomed to the change in time. But how do we remember which Sunday of the year we are supposed to set the clock forward and which Sunday we must set it back? There is a very simple seasonal rule: on the last Sunday in April, we *spring* forward; on the last Sunday in October, we *fall* back.

An old-fashioned Monday washday

Blue Monday

They that wash on Monday
    have all the week to dry;
They that wash on Tuesday
    have let a day go by;
They that wash on Wednesday
    are not so much to blame;
They that wash on Thursday
    wash for very shame. . . .
Author Unknown

Why do so many of us get the "Monday morning blues"? And what are the blues anyway?

The blues are a feeling of sadness, of low spirits. In music, they are sung or played in a minor key that expresses yearning or disappointment. Even the color blue is supposed to have a depressing effect on some people. This is surprising, for it is the color of the sky and the sea in fair weather.

There are several theories as to why Monday is often a "blue" day. Students of social history tell us that it is because, in the past, Monday was always washday. After the old-fashioned Saturday night bath, everybody put on fresh clothing on Sunday. So the week's accumulation of dirty clothes, bed linens, and table linens awaited the housewife on Monday morning.

In the days before washing machines, electricity, or even running water, washday was the worst day of the week. Water had to be hauled in heavy buckets from a pump, well, or even a nearby stream. It had to be heated in cauldrons on a wood- or coal-heated stove or over an outdoor fire. Knuckles were skinned raw as the clothes were scrubbed with a large bar of harsh laundry soap and then rubbed on a ribbed washboard to remove the dirt. Next, the soap had to be rinsed out and the wash had to be wrung dry by hand.

Often, before being hung on the clothesline to dry, items such as shirts, blouses, tablecloths, and napkins had to be starched. This gave them body and stiffness. Sometimes bluing was added to the starchy water, too. The blue dye brightened white clothes and linens that had begun to yellow with age. It is even possible that there is a connection between the use of bluing on washday and the term "blue Monday."

People in many parts of the world still work very hard at washing their clothes. Often they must stand knee-deep in a chilly stream, slapping their garments against the rocks to remove the dirt. But for those of us who use home washing machines or neighborhood Laundromats, Monday doesn't really have to be "blue" any longer.

Yet the Monday morning blues, sometimes called the Monday morning "blahs," seem to hang on. Another reason, of course, is that Monday is the first day of the work or school week for most of us. Scientists tell us that, after a weekend change in routine, our "internal body clocks" are out of harmony. We have lost the rhythm of the previous week.

We might say, in fact, that the cause of so many of our

Monday morning troubles is that Monday comes right after Sunday.

According to the Bible, even God did not declare Monday to be a "good" day. The Book of Genesis tells us that, after making each of the other days of the week, God "saw" that his work was "good" and that he blessed the seventh day. But Monday, the second day, did not receive this mark of approval. As a result, some people believe Monday to be an unlucky day. They will not make important decisions or major changes in their lives on that day.

The Old Testament of the Bible also tells us that the second day was the day on which God made the heavens. So it is not surprising that when the Romans got around to giving names to the days of the week, they named the second day after the moon.

The Greeks, from whom the Romans took so many of their ideas, had a moon goddess called Selene. She was the sister of Helios, the sun god, for whom Sunday was named. A Greek legend about Selene attempts to explain why on some nights the moon cannot be seen.

Selene fell in love with a handsome young shepherd named Endymion who lived on a mountaintop in Greece. Zeus, the ruler of the gods of ancient Greece, scolded the goddess for loving a mortal. So Selene pleaded that Endymion should be given immortality.

Her wish was granted on one condition. Endymion would never grow old, he would never die, but he would lie asleep forever. Therefore, the legend tells us, the sky is dark on certain nights because the moon goddess has gone to visit her lover, who lies sleeping on his mountaintop.

The Romans, too, had a moon goddess whom they called Diana. She was also the goddess of the hunt. But it was said that sometimes Diana used the crescent moon for a bow and sent forth a spray of silvery moonbeams instead of arrows.

The Latin word for moon is *luna*, so Monday to the ancient Romans was *dies lunae*, day of the moon. This explains why most Romance languages — tongues that come from Latin — have these words for Monday:

> French — lundi
> Italian — lunedì
> Spanish — lunes
> Romanian — luni

Portuguese is also a Romance language. But its word for Monday is *segunda-feira*, or second day. Hebrew, Arabic, Greek, and other languages also call Monday second day, as in the Bible.

In Anglo-Saxon, or Old English, the word for the day of the moon is *monandaeg*. We can easily see how this word became *Monday* in modern English. Similar words for Monday in modern northern European tongues are:

> German — Montag
> Dutch — Maandag
> Danish — mandag
> Norwegian — mandag
> Swedish — måndag

No matter what language we use in speaking of the moon, many people are very superstitious about this heavenly body. The reason, perhaps, is because the moon, as we see it, is ever-changing. One phase soon gives way to another, making the moon seem somehow unreliable. In Shakespeare's play *Romeo and Juliet*, Juliet begs Romeo not to swear his love by "the moon, the inconstant moon." She tells him that she fears his love may "prove likewise variable."

The very words *lunacy* and *lunatic* come from the Latin *luna*. It was once believed that insanity was caused by the changes in the moon and that sleeping in the moonlight or gazing too long at the moon could affect the mind.

Nowadays, some police and hospital workers say that there are more accidents and more crimes committed during the full moon than at other times of the month. Many official reports deny this, and also tell us that there is no scientific reason for such a coincidence. Yet, we know that the tides rise and fall in response to the moon. Dogs, wolves, and other animals bark or bay at the full moon. So perhaps there

Wolves baying at the moon after which Monday is sometimes thought to be "unluckily" named

is some effect on humans after all. And perhaps, too, that is another reason why people think Monday is a trifle unlucky. It is, after all, the day of the week that is named for the moon.

On the other hand, there is nothing nicer than a Monday holiday. It means that Sunday isn't the end of the weekend, and it gives many people who don't work on Saturday a three-day vacation.

One holiday that has always been observed on a Monday in the United States and Canada is *Labor Day*. It was first celebrated in 1882 with a parade in New York City to honor working people. Labor Day has been a federal holiday since 1894. All of the states hold it on the first Monday in September. Back in the days when a Monday was almost never a day off from work, labor was very honored indeed by this tribute.

Coming in early September, Labor Day also marks the end of the summer vacation period for many of us. It is around the time of this holiday that the opening of the school year usually takes place. We should note, however, that the traditional day for honoring labor in many other parts of the world, including Europe, Latin America, and China, is May 1.

It took a long time for the United States federal government to get around to deciding that there should be more Monday holidays. But in 1968 a bill was passed that created four more of them. The purpose was to give federal employees additional three-day weekends and to encourage state and local governments and private businesses to do the same for their employees.

Where did the new Monday holidays come from? They came from older holidays that used to fall on a different day of the week each year. Here is a list of the four Monday holidays that went into effect in 1971:

Washington's Birthday was publicly celebrated as early as the 1780s, when George Washington, the first president of the United States, was still alive. Some people observed it on February 11. That was Washington's date of birth on the calendar in use in 1732, the year he was born. Others celebrated it on February 22. That was the equivalent date on the calendar we use today, which England and the American colonies adopted in 1752. Later, February 22 became a legal holiday throughout the United States.

In 1971, however, Washington's birthday was moved to the third Monday in February. Some states call this holiday *Presidents' Day* and some call it *Washington-Lincoln Day*. Sometimes it does fall in between February 12, Abraham Lincoln's date of birth, and February 22, thus linking the two presidents' birthdays. But not always.

Historians may shudder at Washington's birthday having been shifted away from his actual birthdate. But most people seem to accept its being changed to a Monday. They enjoy having a long weekend for leisure, entertainment, travel, or even shopping.

Memorial Day also became a Monday holiday in 1971. Federal offices observe it on the last Monday in May. As of 1984, however, there were still eight states that celebrated Memorial Day on its traditional date, May 30. Various southern states have had their own dates of observance.

Memorial Day began in 1868, shortly after the Civil War,

as a day for decorating the graves of the war dead with flowers and flags. For this reason, it was also called Decoration Day.

Nowadays all who have died serving their country are honored on this day. Just as Labor Day seems to mark the end of summer, the Memorial Day weekend signals the beginning of warm weather and vacation activities. In many parts of the country, the beaches open officially on this weekend.

Memorial Day is the Monday holiday when many beaches and pools open for the summer

Columbus Day, or October 12, is another famous date in history that has been moved. It is now federally observed on the second Monday in October. It commemorates, of course, the discovery of America in 1492. The first United States celebration of this event took place on its 300th anniversary, in 1792, in New York City.

However, the only territory of the United States on which Columbus ever set foot is Puerto Rico. There, and elsewhere in Spanish-speaking America, Columbus is still honored on October 12. The holiday is known as the Day of the Race because of the Spanish heritage he brought to America's shores.

Most states have followed the federal government in making Columbus Day a Monday holiday. But some communities still reserve October 12. Either way, the day is marked by a parade to honor America's discoverer who was, of course, Italian by birth.

The second Monday in October is also a holiday in Canada. There it is Thanksgiving Day. Canada's harvest festival is celebrated earlier in the fall than that of the United States. One reason for this is Canada's more northerly climate.

Veterans' Day was originally called Armistice Day. It was first observed in the United States after the signing of the World War I peace treaty, or armistice, on November 11, 1918. In 1954, the holiday was renamed Veterans' Day to honor all men and women who served in the armed forces.

Since 1971, Veterans' Day is a federal holiday on the fourth Monday in October. Whether it is observed then or on the traditional date of November 11, it is marked by parades, speeches, and special services at war memorials throughout the country.

Celebrating the birthday of Martin Luther King, Jr., an addition to the list of Monday holidays

Newest of the Monday holidays is the *Birthday of Martin Luther King, Jr.* In 1983, the federal government decreed that, starting in 1986, it should be observed on the third Monday in January.

The black civil rights leader and Nobel Peace Prize winner was actually born on January 15, 1929. Since his assassination on April 4, 1968, many states have put aside a special day to honor his memory. Martin Luther King's birthday adds January to the growing list of months that now have Monday holidays in them.

Doing Tuesday's chore with a flat iron in the days before electric irons

And Tuesday, Too

Cut your nails on Monday,
cut them for wealth
Cut your nails on Tuesday,
cut them for health
Author Unknown

Monday's child is fair of face
Tuesday's child is full of grace
Author Unknown

The old folk rhymes seem to be telling us that Tuesday is a pretty good day. But there are probably some people who would disagree.

Back in the days when Monday was washday, Tuesday was ironing day. It was only a little better than Monday. There were no wrinkle-free fabrics or automatic clothes dryers. The Monday wash that came off the clothesline was usually stiff, hard, and crisscrossed with creases.

Before the day's ironing could even begin, most clothing and household linens had to be sprinkled with water. Then they were rolled up tightly and wrapped in towels so that the dampness would seep through completely.

Electric irons were not invented until around 1900. And they didn't come into general use until quite a bit later. The old-fashioned flat irons, as they were called, had to be heated on the stove or on the fireplace hearth. The housewife used two or more flat irons. As one cooled, it was put back to heat and another was taken from the stove. The irons were actually made of iron and so were very heavy. They might weigh ten pounds or more. Their weight helped to press out the wrinkles. Sometimes, though, if an iron was too hot it would leave an ugly scorch mark on the cloth or even burn through it entirely.

Many garments and linens had frills and ruffles. Blouses and shirts had long sleeves that billowed or were fancily shaped. So there were special smaller-sized ironing boards to help get the finishing touches just right. By the end of a long, hot Tuesday, the housewife's arms ached from lifting the heavy irons, her back ached from standing over the ironing board, and her feet were sore and burning. She certainly did not consider Tuesday one of the better days of the week.

Real improvements in Tuesday's chores began to take place around the 1950s. Along came electric steam irons that could also spray the clothes, so they didn't need to be dampened first. Even better were drip-dry, permanent-press, and other "miracle" fabrics that didn't need any ironing at all. Nowadays, almost nobody has to spend all of Tuesday pressing the wrinkles out of a pile of ironing from Monday's wash. And Tuesday really does seem to be a pretty good day.

If Sunday was named for the sun and Monday for the moon, where did Tuesday get its name? Like the other days of the week, it was first named by the Romans. They decided that this day should honor Mars, the god of war.

Mars was also the father of Romulus and Remus. According to legend, Romulus and Remus were twin brothers. As

Tuesday's Roman god, Mars, and the wolf who cared for his twin babes, Romulus and Remus

infants, they were cast adrift on the river, but were rescued and cared for by a wolf. They later grew up to become the founders of Rome.

As the father of Romulus and Remus, Mars was in a sense the grandfather of the Roman people. So they did indeed have a good reason for naming the third day of the week *dies martis,* or the day of the war god. They also named the month of March and the planet Mars after this well-liked god.

The word *Martian* comes from Mars and so does the word *martial.* Martial music is usually bold, stirring, and warlike. *Martial law* means "military law," the kind that is imposed in time of war or other forms of public emergency.

It is not surprising that the word for Tuesday in most Romance languages comes directly from the Latin *dies martis:*

French — mardi
Italian — martedì
Spanish — martes
Romanian — marti

But Portuguese is again an exception. Just as in the case of Monday, Tuesday has a number instead of a name. The Portuguese call it *terça-feira*, or third day. Tuesday is also a numbered day in other tongues, including Greek, Arabic, and Hebrew.

In English, however, just as in Latin, Tuesday means the day of the war god. But the day is named for the ancient Scandinavian god of war. He was called Tyr or Tiw.

Like the Romans, the Scandinavians — or Norsemen, as they were also known — had many gods and goddesses. Both of these ancient peoples believed in a king or ruler of the gods, a queen, a god of thunder, a goddess of youth and beauty, and many others. But although the gods of Roman and Norse mythology often played similar roles, their names were different. And so were the myths surrounding them. Like Mars, Tyr has a wolf in his story. But the stories of the two war gods are unlike in many other ways.

According to legend, the Scandinavian or Norse gods lived somewhere in the sky, in a kingdom called Asgard. A bridge in the form of a rainbow made it possible for the gods to visit the earth. Surprisingly, life in Asgard was not always happy and peaceful. The city of the gods was filled with terror by Fenrir, a fierce and savage wolf that prowled its streets.

A strong chain was forged, but the gods could not think of a way of placing it around Fenrir's neck. At last they came up with a plan. They would use trickery. Fenrir trusted Tyr, who sometimes fed him meat from the tip of his sword. The courageous god of war offered to place his right hand between the wolf's jaws while he was being chained. And so the wolf was made captive.

However, when the angry Fenrir found that he could not tear free of the chain, he bit off Tyr's hand. Tyr's act of sacrifice earned the gratitude of all of Asgard. Perhaps this is why those who worshipped the Norse gods chose to honor Tyr with a day of his own.

The Anglo-Saxon, or Old English, word for Tyr's day was *tiwesdaeg*. The name changed gradually over the centuries to become *Tuesday*. Other modern languages of northern Europe say Tuesday this way:

German — Dienstag
Dutch — Dinsdag
Danish — tirsdag
Norwegian — tirsdag
Swedish — tisdag

Holidays that always fall on Tuesday are rather few in number. But there is one Christian religious holiday that is lively, colorful, and filled with delicious things to eat. It is called Shrove Tuesday and it comes just before the beginning of Lent.

Lent is a period of prayer and fasting that lasts forty days, not including Sundays, until Easter Sunday. It is a time of sacrifice and sadness because it marks the forty days Jesus fasted in the desert and the events that led up to his death. Christians show their sorrow by asking forgiveness for their sins. Often they deny themselves certain favorite foods during Lent. So the Tuesday before Lent begins is a last chance for merrymaking and rich eating.

Other names for Shrove Tuesday, or "confession" Tuesday, are Pancake Tuesday, Doughnut Tuesday, and Fat Tuesday. In the old days, people tried to use up all the butter and other fats in the household. So they ate buttery pancakes, deep-fried doughnuts, and all sorts of sweet, crisp fritters.

Fat Tuesday is really the English translation of *Mardi Gras*.

Celebrating Mardi Gras, or Fat Tuesday

This well-known celebration is also called Carnival. It was introduced to New Orleans, Louisiana, by French colonists. Some cities in the southern United States and in Latin America have Mardi Gras festivities that start in January or February and go on for weeks. There are street parades with gaily decorated floats, masquerade parties, and huge fancy-dress balls. But no matter how early in the season the Mardi Gras revelries may have begun, they always end on Shrove Tuesday. Like Easter Sunday, Shrove Tuesday is a movable feast. So we must check the calendar each year to find out on which Tuesday in late winter it will occur.

A very different kind of Tuesday holiday is *Election Day*. Since 1845, the president of the United States has been elected on the Tuesday after the first Monday in November. Presidential elections, of course, take place every four years. But state and local elections are held on that Tuesday in the in-between years as well.

On the other hand, there are certain kinds of elections that may take place on other days of the week and at other times of the year. These include so-called "special elections" to fill an office that has been unexpectedly vacated in the middle of a term. They also include primary elections for nominating the candidates who will later run in the final election.

As there are so few Tuesday holidays, it would be a pity to lose one. Yet a bill introduced in the United States Congress in 1983 called for changing the regular Tuesday Election Day to a Sunday. As Sunday is already a holiday for most people, this idea does not seem to have been very popular. So far nothing more has been done toward making such a change.

Mercury, the god who gave the Romans their name for Wednesday

Wednesday in the Middle

Wednesday's child is full of woe
Thursday's child has far to go

Wednesday's child is sour and sad
Thursday's child is merry and glad
Authors Unknown

Monday for wealth,
Tuesday for health,
Wednesday the best day of all . . .
Author Unknown

Is Wednesday good or bad, lucky or unlucky? People who are superstitious about the days of the week say that it is neither. It is a neutral day. Perhaps this is because, as the fourth day of seven, it falls exactly in the middle of the week. Wednesday is just halfway from the beginning and halfway to the end.

The German word for Wednesday, in fact, is *Mittwoch* or "midweek." And in Yiddish, which has similar names for most of the days, it is *mitvoch*. Russian, Polish, Czech, Serbo-Croatian, and Hungarian have their own group of similar-sounding words all meaning "middle." It is as though people are breathing a small sigh of relief that the week is at least half over.

Where then did Wednesday get its name? It comes from Odin, the ruler of the Scandinavian, or Norse, gods. He is also known as Woden or Wotan.

Odin lived in the great palace of Valhalla in the mythical city of Asgard. He was the father of Tyr and other gods and also of creatures who were half-god, half-mortal. He held supreme power over life on earth. The Norse peoples believed that heroes who died in battle were brought to Valhalla, where they enjoyed a glorious afterlife. Their wounds were miraculously healed and they spent their days in sumptuous feasting.

Odin had a deep craving for knowledge and wisdom. He rode about on a swift, powerful horse that had eight legs, four in front and four in back. Two ravens perched on his shoulders. Each day they flew to earth and returned with news of what was happening. His search for wisdom was so great that, according to legend, it cost him an eye.

As he often did, Odin disguised himself as an old man and went to drink from the well of wisdom. But he was recognized by Mimir, the giant who guarded the well. Mimir demanded that Odin should first make a great sacrifice. So the ruler of the gods tore one of his eyes from its socket and allowed Mimir to cast it deep into the well.

It may seem strange that a god with such power should have been forced to bend to the will of even a giant. But according to the Norse myths the gods had a number of weaknesses and failings. In some ways they were portrayed as being almost human. So, like his son Tyr who lost a hand, Odin lost an eye. But he did gain great wisdom. His sacrifice, like Tyr's, was felt to be noble and courageous.

The Anglo-Saxon, or Old English, word for the day of Odin,

or Woden, was *wodnesdaeg*. This word of course became *Wednesday* in modern English. German, too, had a name for Wednesday that meant "Woden's day" before it was changed to *Mittwoch*. But other modern Germanic and Scandinavian languages still call this day after the one-eyed ruler of the gods:

Dutch — Woensdag
Danish — onsdag
Norwegian — onsdag
Swedish — onsdag

The Romans, the first to give names to the days, chose a different god to honor on the fourth day of the week. They picked Mercury, who was the swift-footed messenger of the gods. This busy youth wore a winged cap and had wings on his heels. Because he could move about so speedily, he was also the god of travel and commerce, and even of thieves.

Mercury carried a wand around which two fighting snakes were magically entwined in friendship. It was topped with a pair of wings. This wand, called a "caduceus," is thought to have been a symbol of healing. In modern times, it has been adopted as a medical emblem. Messenger and other rapid-delivery services often use insignia that show a fleet, running figure of the god Mercury.

Dies mercurii, or the day of Mercury, was the ancient Roman word for Wednesday. The planet Mercury was also named for this god. And so was the fluid white metal, called either mercury or quicksilver, that is used to fill thermometers. Mercury is the only metal that is liquid at ordinary temperatures. When we speak of somebody being mercurial, we usually mean on-the-go, changeable, and restless, like the ever-moving god Mercury.

Most of the Romance languages have names for Wednesday that are taken from the Latin *dies mercurii* of the ancient Romans:

French — mercredi
Italian — mercoledì
Spanish — miércoles
Romanian — miercuri

Portuguese, however, sticks to its pattern of numbering the days, so Wednesday is *quarto-feira,* or fourth day. The Hebrew, Arabic, and Greek words for Wednesday also mean "fourth day."

Wednesday's position in the middle of the week makes it an excellent day for "breaking up" one's work schedule. Some people are actually lucky enough to be able to take a half or even a full day off on Wednesday. This leaves only two more work days until the weekend. In the theater, Wednesday is usually the only weekday on which a matinee, or afternoon performance, is given. So a visit to a play or other entertain-

Wednesday is often matinee day

ment can offer a pleasant midweek break from the daily routine.

There are, however, no legal holidays that regularly fall on Wednesday. The best-known religious holiday on that day is Ash Wednesday.

Ash Wednesday comes directly after Shrove Tuesday and is the first day of Lent, the Christian season of sorrow and repentance. Many people attend church services on that day, and Roman Catholics usually have their foreheads smeared with a bit of ash in the form of a cross.

This practice arose about 1,400 years ago, or 600 years after the death of Jesus Christ. At first only the foreheads of convicted criminals were marked with this sign. The grayish smudge was intended to be a reminder that "dust thou art, and unto dust shalt thou return."

These words from the Book of Genesis are really telling us that the life of the body is temporary and that one must prepare oneself for death. Soon other Christians wanted to express regret for their sins by kneeling before a priest or other church official and receiving a marking of ash. The ashes used on Ash Wednesday come from the burning of the palms that were blessed on the Palm Sunday of the year before.

The name Lent comes from *lencten,* an Old English word meaning lengthening of the days, or springtime. So we know that Ash Wednesday, the first day of Lent, arrives toward the beginning of spring. But, as the holidays of the Easter season occur on different dates each year, we must check the calendar to find out on which Wednesday in February or March it will take place.

Jupiter, the Roman god of thundery Thursday

Thundery Thursday

And if I loved you Wednesday,
   Well, what is that to you?
I do not love you Thursday —
   So much is true.
      Edna St. Vincent Millay: from *Thursday*

Thursday come, and the week is gone.
      George Herbert: *Jacula Prudentum*

Thursday may be a bad day for those who have given their hearts to a fickle lover, one whose feelings change from day to day. Or Thursday may be a happy harbinger of the week's drawing to a close. Thursday's name, however, tells us that it is the day of the thunder god, a powerful hammer-throwing charioteer from the mythical realm of Asgard.

The name of the Norse thunder god was Thor. Like Tyr, for whom Tuesday is named, Thor was a son of Odin. The wheels of Thor's chariot crossing the sky were said to create the deep rumble of thunder that was heard on earth. The chariot itself was drawn by two goats whose galloping hoofs struck sparks.

In addition, Thor had a magic hammer. When he threw the hammer, it caused lightning to flash across the sky and stab the earth. But Thor's hammer always came back to him so that he could aim its terrifying bolts again and again.

Thor's strength and boldness made him a brave match for the giants that often threatened Asgard and its inhabitants. One of the legends about Thor tells how the giant Thrym stole Thor's magic hammer and refused to return it unless the goddess Freya would marry him.

The beautiful blond Freya was the goddess of love and beauty. The gods could not bear to see her leave Asgard for the land of the giants. So with the help of Loki, the cunning god of mischief, Thor devised a plot to trick Thrym.

Thor disguised himself as the goddess Freya, and Loki dressed himself as Freya's bridesmaid. Together they traveled to Thrym's castle where a great wedding feast was being held. The "bride" astonished Thrym by devouring an entire ox, eating eight large whole fish, and drinking several barrels of wine. But the sly Loki calmed Thrym's suspicions by telling him that Freya had been too excited to eat for a whole week before the wedding.

At the close of the feast, Loki told Thrym that he must now place the stolen hammer in the lap of the bride, Freya. The trusting giant did so. At once Thor leaped up, threw off his disguise, and slew Thrym with his hammer. This is the way Thor regained his hammer and lightning was returned to the heavens and to the earth.

The Old English name *thursdaeg* became *Thursday* in modern English. Scandinavian tongues also call this day after Thor. But Germanic languages really call it "thunder day" because of Thor's role as the god of thunder. *Donner* in German and *donder* in Dutch mean "thunder":

German — Donnerstag
Dutch — Donderdag
Danish — torsdag
Norwegian — torsdag
Swedish — torsdag

The Romans, too, named the fifth day of the week after a god who could streak the skies with lightning and make them vibrate with thunder. His name was Jupiter. He was also the ruler of the gods and of the earth, like Odin in Norse mythology.

Jupiter's symbols were an eagle, a sign of his all-seeing power, and a handful of arrowlike shafts of lightning. When an ancient Roman sneezed, those closest to the sneezer said, "Jupiter preserve you," just as we now say, "God bless you." The Romans named the largest planet in the solar system Jupiter, after this supreme god.

Another word for Jupiter was *Jove*. "By Jove!" is an expression of agreeable surprise that comes from the name of the Roman god. So does the word *jovial*, meaning "merry and hearty." And the Latin words *dies jovis* mean, "Jove's day."

Dies jovis has given us these words for Thursday in the Latin-based languages:

French — jeudi
Italian — giovedì (pronounced *joh-vay-DEE*)
Spanish — jueves
Romanian — joi

Quinta-feira, or fifth day, is the Portuguese word for Thursday. And this day is also numbered rather than named in Greek, Hebrew, Arabic, and other languages.

Thursdays, like the other days of the week, mean certain things to certain people. Among Moslems, members of the Islamic faith, Friday is the week's holy day. So Thursday afternoon is a time of preparation for this day of rest and prayer. People often give donations to the poor and visit the graves of their relatives on Thursdays.

Thursday evenings are also a popular time for weddings, as the bride, groom, and wedding guests will be able to enjoy a Friday holiday. Similarly, in Christian societies, Saturday nights are often favored for weddings because of Sunday's being a holiday. The prophet Mohammed, founder of the Islamic religion, is believed to have been married on a Thursday. So this is another reason for this tradition among followers of the faith of Islam.

Like Monday, which was once washday, and Tuesday, which used to be ironing day, Thursday once had its special household chore. About a hundred years ago, in the United States and Canada, it was known as "sweeping day."

In the late 1800s and early 1900s, the fashion was for houses to be furnished with overstuffed sofas and easy chairs, ornately carved wood, thick rugs, heavy draperies, and many ornaments. All of these items were great "dust collectors."

The electric vacuum cleaner was not invented until around 1900, and it was many more years before it came into general use. Numerous homes did not even have electricity at the turn of the century. So the housewife or the maidservant spent all of Thursday trying to pound the dust out of the furniture and hangings. The rugs themselves were often picked up and taken out to the yard to be beaten. Finally the walls, mirrors, pictures, and all the curios and bric-a-brac were whisked with a long feather duster.

After an exhausting Thursday, everything was put back in place. Unfortunately, however, most of the dust that had been attacked on "sweeping day," still hovered in the air and soon settled again. For it hadn't *gone* anywhere. It had only been stirred up and moved around. No wonder the vacuum cleaner was so welcome when it finally came on the scene. It actually collected the dust!

We may be surprised that there was so much dust to worry about in the "good old days," because we tend to think of them as having been free of air pollution. But that wasn't the case. Factory chimneys, drying animal manure, coal- and wood-burning stoves, and sewer gas all filled the air with soot, cinders, other filth, and bad odors as well.

The two best-known holidays that always take place on a Thursday happen to commemorate famous feasts. The first of these recalls the Last Supper. This meal was shared by Jesus Christ and his twelve disciples in Jerusalem on the Thursday evening before Good Friday, the day on which Christ died.

The day of the Last Supper is known as Holy Thursday or Maundy Thursday. The name Maundy is believed to come from the Latin words *dies mandate*, or "day of the mandate." For, according to the Bible, it was on that Thursday that Christ mandated, or commanded, his disciples "that ye love one another."

As a symbol of his own brotherly love, Christ washed the feet of the twelve disciples at the Last Supper. Later it became a widespread practice for Roman Catholic emperors, kings, nobles, and wealthy landowners, as well as bishops and priests, to wash the feet of the poor on Maundy Thursday. Often twelve or thirteen servants, beggars, pilgrims, or other wanderers were chosen. The kneeling noble or church official would bathe the feet of the less fortunate to show that he accepted Christ's teaching that all men are brothers.

Another historic feast that is nowadays recalled on a Thursday in the United States is Thanksgiving. The first Thanksgiving, of course, took place at Plymouth, Massachusetts in the autumn of 1621 and lasted three days. The Pilgrim settlers were grateful indeed for having survived their first terrible winter in the New World. With the help of the Indians, they had learned to plant corn, beans, pumpkins, and squash, to hunt venison and bear, dig for clams, and fish the rivers. So it was these foods plus the wild turkey, all of them native to New England, that made up the menu for the first Thanksgiving dinner.

The idea of having a yearly harvest festival of celebration and prayer continued, especially in New England. But each town or other community picked its own day. Sometimes the reasons were rather surprising. Desserts like Indian pudding and apple, mince, and pumpkin pie were considered very important for a proper Thanksgiving feast. But these dishes required molasses from the West Indies for sweetening and often raisins and spices from even more distant places. So, if a shipment was late in reaching port in New England, some towns simply postponed the day for their Thanksgiving dinner until the ingredients for all the holiday goodies were on hand.

At last, in 1863, President Abraham Lincoln recom-

The Indians sharing their bounty with Pilgrims for the first Thanksgiving feast

mended that Thanksgiving Day should be a national holiday and it should take place on the last Thursday in November. This observance continued until 1939. In that year, there happened to be five Thursdays in November. So President Franklin Roosevelt proclaimed that Thanksgiving should be held one week earlier, on November 23, the fourth Thursday, rather than November 30, the last Thursday.

His reason was that the country was in a severe economic depression. The Christmas shopping season began right after Thanksgiving. If there were more shopping days to Christmas, businesses would take in more money and be able to give jobs to more people.

Thanksgiving, a well-loved Thursday holiday in the United States

The policy of having Thanksgiving a week earlier continued for the next two years. But in those years there were only four Thursdays in November. Some states refused to go along with Roosevelt's plan, and many people became very confused about when to have Thanksgiving. So in 1941 Congress ruled that, starting the following year, Thanksgiving would always be observed on the fourth Thursday in November.

For many of us, this popular Thursday holiday offers a bonus. Most schools and many offices and businesses remain closed on the Friday after Thanksgiving, presenting us with the pleasant prospect of a four-day weekend.

Just after sunset on Friday, the Jewish Sabbath begins

Friday, Fair or Fearsome

I let him know his name should be
Friday, which was the day I saved
his life.
          Daniel Defoe: *Robinson Crusoe*

I had that fellow Friday
Just to keep the tavern tidy.
          Charles Edward Carryl: *Robinson Crusoe*

Friday has been called both the luckiest and the unluckiest day of the week. It was certainly lucky for Robinson
Crusoe. This famous character in the story by Daniel Defoe
was marooned on a desert island. But he found that he was
not entirely alone there. He met another man whom he saved
from being eaten by cannibals and who became his trusted
friend and servant. Robinson Crusoe named this man Friday because that was the day on which he rescued him from
death. It was a lucky day, of course, for Friday as well!

When we speak nowadays of a "man Friday" or a "girl
Friday," we mean an all-around assistant, usually in a business office or similar setting. The term *"girl* Friday," however, is considered rather belittling to women. We don't speak
of a *"boy* Friday." So perhaps, if we are going to say "man
Friday," we should also say "woman Friday." Maybe the

whole idea of having a personal assistant with servantlike duties was better suited to Robinson Crusoe's day, the 1700s, than to our own.

For most of us, whatever our occupation, Friday is the last day of the work or school week. The weekend with its chance for a change of pace lies ahead. From this happy prospect comes the catchy expression "T.G.I.F." The initials stand for, "Thank God it's Friday."

And indeed some people choose Friday evening as a time for going out in groups or for having a T.G.I.F. party at somebody's home. At the same time, police records tell us that there is an increase in auto accidents on Friday nights and also in robberies and burglaries. In some cases, the pent-up energies of the work week seem to explode with an unfortunate bang on Friday.

Many people, though, feel that Friday is the luckiest day of the week. This is because of what is written about it in the Old Testament of the Bible. The Book of Genesis relates that it was on the sixth day that God created human life. He was so pleased with his work that he pronounced the day as being "very good." Most of the other days God had simply called "good."

On the other hand, those who feel Friday is the unluckiest day point to the fact that Jesus Christ died on a Friday. Oddly, Christians call this day Good Friday. But it is thought that the original name for it was God's Friday. As time went on, Friday became "hangman's day" in many countries. Criminals who were executed on that day would have been surprised indeed by today's expression, "Thank God it's Friday."

*

Friday takes its name from the Norse goddess Frigga. She was the wife of Odin, the ruler of the gods. Like the other immortals who lived in the heavenly city of Asgard, Frigga had divine powers. At the same time, like many of the other gods, she sometimes made serious blunders such as any ordinary human might make.

One of the saddest stories about Frigga is the death of her beloved son Balder. This god of brightness and beauty was a young man who was believed to represent summer. He was therefore precious to all of the northern peoples, for their season of warmth and sunshine was all too short.

To ensure Balder's life, Frigga traveled the earth and made every animal, plant, stick, and stone promise never to harm Balder. Fire, disease, and other evils also pledged that they would forever remain harmless to Balder, through Frigga's power. She forgot only one thing — a mistletoe plant that grew on an oak tree near the great palace of Valhalla.

Loki, the god of mischief, was sometimes helpful to the gods, but he could also be very evil. He hated Balder, whom everyone loved so. Disguising himself as an old woman, he learned from Frigga that she had failed to get a promise from the mistletoe plant not to harm Balder. With wicked cunning, Loki plucked the mistletoe from the oak tree and fashioned a sharp-tipped dart from it. Then he guided the hand of Balder's blind brother, Hoder, so that Hoder hurled it at Balder.

The dart pierced Balder and he died instantly. Despite Frigga's efforts, he could not be restored to life. Many believe that in this Norse legend the blind, grim, and silent Hoder represents winter in its victory over summer.

Frigga, the Norse goddess for whom Friday is named, with her beloved son Balder, as a baby

As the wife of Odin, Frigga was the goddess of marriage and the household. But her role is closely related to that of Freya, the youthful goddess of love and beauty and also of fertility, or childbearing. It is thought that, among some of the peoples of northern Europe, the two goddesses may have blended into one.

For example, the Anglo-Saxon, or Old English, name for Friday is *frigedaeg*, or Frigga's day. But some other names for Friday in modern Germanic and Scandinavian tongues seem a bit closer to Freya than Frigga:

German — Freitag
Dutch — Vrijdag
Danish — fredag
Norwegian — fredag
Swedish — fredag

There is no question that the ancient Romans named Friday for Venus, who was *their* goddess of love and beauty. Venus was believed to have risen from the foam of the sea. She became the mother of Cupid, a pudgy winged little boy who acted as the god of love. It was believed that anyone whose heart was pierced with one of Cupid's arrows would fall forever and hopelessly in love.

The Romans kept to their pattern of naming the planets after their favorite gods and goddesses. So, like Mars, Mercury, and Jupiter, Venus, too, had a planet named for her. Her day of the week in Latin was *dies veneris*, or the day of Venus. The following Latin-based languages have these similar names for Friday:

French - vendredi
Italian - venerdì
Spanish - viernes
Romanian - vineri

As Friday is the sixth day of the week, counting from Sunday, the Portuguese call it just that: *sexta-feira*. Arabic, which usually numbers the days, has a special name for Friday that means "day of gathering."

All devout Moslems say prayers five times a day every day of the week. They pray at dawn, noon, afternoon, evening, and nightfall. Prayers need not be said in a mosque, which is the house of religious worship for Moslems. They may be said at home, in the fields, in some quiet spot in the middle of a bustling city, almost anywhere at all.

But Friday, the Moslem holy day, is different. On that day, there is a call to noon prayer in the mosque. The congregation also listens to a sermon given by the imam, or preacher. In preparation for the Friday holy-day "gathering," people bathe carefully and dress in their best clothes. Moslems are permitted to conduct business before and after the Friday service. But many choose to enjoy Friday as their weekly day of rest. For the next day, Saturday, is the beginning of a brand-new work week.

Members of the Jewish faith, on the other hand, begin their Sabbath on Friday evening at sunset. Their weekly holy day continues until sunset on Saturday. All Jewish holidays start on the evening of the previous day because, according to the Bible, that is how God created the days. The Book of Genesis tells us: "And there was evening and there was morning, one day."

In traditional Jewish homes, the Sabbath is said to be "ushered in like a bride." Early on Friday, the house is made sparkling clean, the Sabbath meal is cooked, and the table is set with a fine cloth and the family's best china, silver, and glassware.

As sunset approaches, the family members, freshly bathed and dressed, assemble for the lighting of the Sabbath candles. They then sit down to a festive meal that celebrates the beginning of the seventh day. The entire twenty-four hours are to be devoted to rest and prayer.

Even the poorest of religious Jewish families have always endeavored to observe the Sabbath as a special time. It is also an act of grace to invite guests to share the Friday evening and other Sabbath meals. Many Jews attend synagogue services on Friday evening and on Saturday as well.

While Friday may be an occasion for festive eating in some faiths, it was for many centuries a fast day for Roman Catholics. This did not mean that people had to abstain from food completely. Eating was permitted. But no meat was to be included in the day's meals. So "fish on Friday" became the usual practice. The reason was that Jesus Christ died on a Friday. "Meatless" Friday was meant as a sign of penance and sacrifice. In 1966, however, the Roman Catholic Church officially lifted the ban on eating meat on Friday.

Good Friday, though, remains a part of the Lenten fasting period. This solemn day specifically commemorates the Friday on which Christ died on the cross. It takes place two days before Easter Sunday, the day on which Christ is believed to have risen from the dead. Some people feel that it is fitting, after all, to call this Friday "good" because of the benefits resulting from Christ's resurrection.

Like the other holidays of the Easter season, the date of Good Friday changes each year. It can occur as early as March 20 and as late as April 23.

There are still a number of people who insist that Friday is a bad luck day. One of the examples they give is Black Friday. This is the name given to two Fridays in the 1800s that saw terrifying financial panics in the United States. The first of these monetary crises, involving banks and the stock market, took place on September 24, 1869, and the second on September 19, 1873.

In this century, the greatest of all stock market crashes occurred in 1929. This event was so disastrous that some people plunged to their death from the windows of their office buildings into the canyons of Wall Street, in New York City's financial district. They felt that suicide was preferable to facing personal ruin and public disgrace.

Yet the day of the 1929 crash, October 29, was not — as might have been expected — another Black Friday. It was instead an innocent-appearing Tuesday.

There is one kind of Friday, however, that always seems to frighten everybody. It is a Friday that happens to fall on the thirteenth day of the month. The reason, again, is believed to stem from the events surrounding the final hours of Jesus Christ. At the Last Supper there were thirteen at table, Christ and the twelve disciples. One of the disciples secretly betrayed Christ and this led to his death on the following day, Friday. Thus, any Friday the thirteenth is thought to be filled with bad omens.

So great is the fear of the number thirteen itself that there is actually a word for it — triskaidekaphobia. This tongue twister, based on Greek-language roots, actually breaks down quite simply to *tris-kai-deka-phobia*, or "three-and-ten fear."

Nobody really knows when thirteen became a scary number. Some say it all began long before the time of Christ. They say it started when human beings first began to count. They added up their ten fingers and their two feet and got as far as twelve. After twelve there was mystery and the terror of the unknown. One wonders, however, why early peoples would not have gone on to count their toes as well.

The ancient Chinese did not think thirteen was a dangerous number. They noted that the moon began its cycle thirteen times a year. This helped them and other early civilizations to make up a lunar, or moon, calendar. The Hebrew calendar is the oldest of the moon calendars still in use today.

Also, there are approximately thirteen weeks in each of the four seasons of the year. There are thirteen stripes in the American flag for the original Thirteen Colonies. And there are thirteen cards in each of the four suits of a pack of playing cards — hearts, clubs, diamonds, and spades. Even this does not seem an especially bad omen, unless of course one is very unlucky at cards.

Yet the fear of thirteen is so great that many tall buildings do not have a floor numbered thirteen. Street addresses often avoid having a thirteen in them. And it is still considered by some to be unlucky for thirteen people to be seated at table. Most airlines are careful not to include a thirteen in their flight or seat numbers, and there are people who won't fly at all on the thirteenth day of the month.

Some people count the steps of a staircase. If there are thirteen of them, they will take the last two in a single jump.

The number thirteen is often avoided because it is thought to be unlucky

After all, back in the days when Friday was "hangman's day," there were usually thirteen steps leading up to the gallows. These were the steps the condemned criminal had to climb after the noose was placed around his neck.

There is, of course, no way to avoid Friday the thirteenth. Each year has at least one such day in it. But some years are worse than others. A year can have as many as three Friday the thirteenths in it. The year 1984 was such a year. Other triple-threat years to look out for are 1987, 1998, 2009, and 2012.

In the years in between, Friday triskaidekaphobes can breathe a little easier. There will be only one or two days each year when a fearsome Friday and the frightening number thirteen come together.

Finally, here is some news for those who suspect that the very first Good Friday may also have been the thirteenth day of the month.

No one has ever known the exact date of the crucifixion, or even been sure of the year. But recently a pair of British scientists have studied this matter carefully. Using astronomical calculations along with evidence from the Bible, they say they are certain that Christ was crucified on Friday, April 3, in the year 33. The day was definitely *not* a Friday the thirteenth.

A festive Saturday night party

Saturday Makes Seven

How pleasant is Saturday night,
When I've tried all the week to be good,
And not said a word that was bad,
And obliged everyone that I could.
   Nancy Dennis Sproat: *Lullabies for Children*

W e often think of Saturday as being a day of reward. The Bible tells us that, after having created the world in six days, God himself rested on the seventh day. That day, of course, became the Sabbath, or holy day, for members of the Jewish faith.

The rewards of Saturday can be simple or sumptuous. Back in the days before modern plumbing, one of the great joys of the week was the Saturday night bath. Farmers, factory workers, and other laborers usually worked six whole days, from Monday through Saturday. Children often attended school six days.

On Saturday night the entire family looked forward to scrubbing away the week's grime and to putting on fresh, clean clothes on Sunday morning. But without running water or an automatic water heater this was no easy matter. As on

Monday washdays, water had to be carried in buckets or pails from a backyard pump or well. It was then heated over a coal or wood fire and poured into a metal bathtub. The tub, which was movable, sometimes had handles for lifting. It was usually placed near the kitchen fire for warmth.

Some tubs were slipper-shaped, wider at the end where one sat and narrower at the opposite end, for one's feet. Some were just round, deep basins that were also used for doing the family wash. The oldtime bathtubs were seldom large enough to recline in. Having a good long soak didn't happen very often either. The water cooled quickly and additional water had to be heated and poured in. Besides, there were other family members waiting their turn. And, in fact, it wasn't at all unusual for the same bath water to be used over and over again.

Nowadays bathing is as simple as turning on a bath or shower tap for many of us. And we can bathe every day if we wish. But getting clean on Saturday night was, and still is, often a preparation for a night out. Friday evening may be a time for letting off steam but Saturday night is the traditional "date night." Large parties, dances, weddings, and other formal celebrations also seem to go hand in hand with Saturday night. The Romans, in fact, named Saturday after a god in whose honor a rollicking festival was held each year. The god was called Saturn. And the revelries named for him were known as the Saturnalia.

Saturn is a god with a strange history. He was the god of time and also the father of Jupiter, the Roman ruler of the heavens and the earth. Saturn had a peculiar habit. He ate his own children. When his sixth and last child was born,

Having a Saturday night bath in an oldtime bathtub

81

his wife, Ops, decided to deceive him. She placed a stone inside a bundle of baby clothes and presented it to Saturn. He promptly swallowed the bundle, stone and all, not realizing he had been tricked.

Meantime, the real child was safely hidden away and grew up to become Jupiter. He then confronted his father and forced him to cast up the other five children. They, too, took their places as important gods and goddesses in Roman mythology.

To better understand the story of Saturn, we need to keep in mind that he was the god who represented time. The act of eating his own children was really a symbol of what time does. It both creates and destroys all life on earth.

Most of the myths of ancient Rome are based on those of the ancient Greeks. So it isn't surprising that Saturn was a Roman version of the Greek god of time, whose name was Cronus. Many English words relating to time come from *Cronus.* Some examples are *chronograph,* a special kind of watch or other time-measuring instrument, and *chronology,* the orderly recording of events by dates. And when we speak of a chronic disease or other condition, we mean one that goes on for a very long time.

The god Saturn differed from the Greek god Cronus, however, in that he played yet another important role in Roman mythology. After he was overthrown by his son Jupiter, he was sent away to the countryside outside Rome. There he became the god of agriculture. He was both a sower and a harvester of grain and other seed plants. His very name, Saturn, is believed to come from the Latin word *sator,* which means "sower."

Saturn was often portrayed with a sickle in one hand and

Saturday's god, Saturn, a sower and harvester of grain

a sheaf of wheat in the other. In fact, the Romans liked him so much as a harvest god that they gave him his own yearly harvest festival. It took place in December and lasted seven days, from the 17th to the 23rd. This celebration was, of course, the Saturnalia.

In one way, the Saturnalia resembled a holiday of thanksgiving. There were religious ceremonies and lavish feasting. Schools were closed and most people didn't go to work. The Saturnalia were also an occasion for exchanging gifts, including small clay figurines of the god Saturn holding his harvester's sickle. There was, too, a wild carnival-like atmosphere. Criminals went without punishment and slaves were allowed to do as they pleased. Some even changed places with their owners and were waited upon by their masters. The final days of the Saturnalia were said to be boisterous and unbridled.

As Saturn was such a popular god, it isn't surprising the Romans named both a day of the week and a planet after him. He ranked with Mars, Mercury, Jupiter, and Venus in having his name given to one of the five planets that were visible to the peoples of ancient times.

The seventh day of the week is the only one that gets its English name from a Roman god rather than a Norse god. *Dies saturni*, or day of Saturn in Latin, became *saeterdaeg* in Anglo-Saxon and *Saturday* in modern English.

Many languages, though, including most Latin-based tongues, have names for Saturday that have nothing at all to do with the god Saturn. They simply follow the writings in the Old Testament of the Bible and call the seventh day "sabbath." Here are some examples:

Italian — sabato
Spanish — sábado
Portuguese — sabado
Romanian — sîmbătă
Polish — sobota
Czech — sobota
Serbo-Croatian — subota
Hungarian — szombat
Russian — subóta
Greek — Sávvato
Arabic — al-sabbt
Hebrew — shabbat
Yiddish — shabbes

The modern Scandinavian languages, too, have a name for the seventh day that refers to the Old Testament Sabbath. Saturday is called "Lord's day":

Danish — lørdag
Norwegian — lørdag
Swedish — lördag

The Dutch word *Zaterdag* is, however, very close to the Anglo-Saxon *saeterdaeg* and the English *Saturday*. We can clearly see the connection with the god Saturn. But what about German and French? Their words for Saturday are somewhat mystifying. They are:

German — Samstag
French — samedi

These names also seem to have something to do with Saturn, even though they may not appear to at first. Saturn, we recall, was the god of agriculture. The German word for seeds, or grain, is *Samen*. So Samstag is really "seed day," or a day to honor the god of sowing and harvesting.

In French, the word for sowing is *semer* and seeds are called *semailles*. So *samedi*, the French word for Saturday, may indeed mean "day of the seed-sower," or the god Saturn.

Lastly, the German language has yet another word for Saturday. It is *Sonnabend*, which means the "eve of Sunday." This reminds us that the Sunday Sabbath of the Christians follows the Saturday Sabbath of the Jews.

The one Saturday of the year that is sacred to all Christians is Holy Saturday. It is the last day of Lent and the final day of Holy Week, which begins with Palm Sunday and ends with the dawn of Easter Sunday. Holy Saturday is also, of course, the day after Good Friday. So it is a day of mourning for Christ's death on the cross.

The day ends, however, on a less sorrowful note. Often special religious services are held and churchgoers eagerly await the first strokes of midnight. The ringing of the chimes announces the joyous news of the rebirth of Christ. And so a sad Holy Saturday gives way to a happy Easter Sunday.

Among Jews, Saturday until sundown is a continuation of the Sabbath day that began at sunset on Friday. In ancient times, strict laws were handed down. Almost every kind of labor was forbidden on this day of rest and prayer. Jews were not to light fires, cook food, clean house, carry burdens, or travel. Even their servants and their animals were to rest, so all journeys had to be on foot and could not be more than about a mile. Many centuries later, in the 1600s, the Puritans of New England adopted similar rules of behavior for their Sunday Sabbath observance.

Those modern-day Jews who are very religious continue to obey the Sabbath restrictions. All food is cooked before sundown on Friday. It is eaten cold on Saturday or kept in a warming oven that does not have to be relit. Even turning on an electric light on the Sabbath is forbidden. It has long been a custom for some Jews to request their non-Jewish neighbors to turn on lamps and light stoves for them. Today's deeply observant Jews will not ride in automobiles or other vehicles or even in elevators on the Sabbath. And they will not handle money or carry purses or wallets.

The Saturday Sabbath ends as reverently as it began with a ceremony that sees the holy day out. Once evening sets in, the new work week arrives. Shops and other businesses that were closed for the Sabbath reopen on Sunday, which is usually a lively shopping day.

"Six days shalt thou labor, and do all they work; but the seventh day is a sabbath unto the Lord thy God. . . ." These words appear in the Book of Exodus of the Old Testament. With Saturday, the seven-day week has been completed. And a new round of days is about to begin.

A hot and sticky "dog day" of summer

Red-Letter and Other Days

The red-letter days, now become,
to all intents and purposes,
dead-letter days.
  Charles Lamb: *Oxford in the Vacation*

Some of the days in our lives are memorable for special reasons. We may not recall what day of the week they fell on. We remember only that they stand out as being exciting, unusual, thrilling, filled with happy surprise.

Such a day would be called a "red-letter day." It might be your birthday, the day you got the lead in the school play, the day you got your first job or received an important promotion.

We may wonder why we call these gala days "red-letter days." The answer goes back to the early centuries of Christianity. It became the practice for the most important festivals on the church calendar to be marked in red lettering. Other days of religious observance that were of lesser importance were lettered in black.

Judging from the quotation from Charles Lamb, the English author of humorous essays must have enjoyed many red-letter days during his stay at the university. But the vacation period was a quiet time. So he coined the term "dead-letter days." Dead letters, of course, are pieces of mail that are never delivered. So a dead-letter day is one in which there are no happy surprises, probably not any sort of news at all.

Other writers of the past have made up their own descriptions of dreary, boring days in which nothing seems to happen. Margaret Fuller was an American lecturer and literary critic who lived in the first half of the 1800s. Brilliant and restless, she traveled to Italy and lived there for some years. One day she wrote in her diary:

> This was one of the rye-bread days,
> all dull and damp without.

If we think of the moist texture and grayish tinge of a slice of rye bread, we know exactly the kind of day Margaret Fuller was talking about.

Speaking of food, there is another kind of day that resembles something we eat:

> My salad days,
> When I was green in judgment.

These lines are from William Shakespeare's play *Antony and Cleopatra*. Ever since they were written, they have seemed a perfect way to express the time of youth and inexperience in our lives. We can almost see the tender shoots and fresh leaves for a green salad poking their way up from the moist earth. And it's easy to compare the young plants with the innocent vigor and bounciness of those years when we are new at life and eager to get on with it.

On the other hand, there is nothing that makes us feel more draggy and tired than a "dog day." Almost everyone has panted through the hot, sultry weather that often arrives around the beginning of July, if not sooner, and that may last through August and even into September.

We generally connect the term "dog days" with the way a gasping, furry animal must feel on such a day. But actually the steamy, sticky weather of high summer gets its name from Sirius, the Dog Star. This star, the brightest in the heavens, happens to rise with the sun for about forty days beginning around July 3. The rising of Sirius has no connection with the soaring of the temperature at that time of year. But the ancient Greeks and many other peoples believed that it did. It is also untrue that dogs are likely to get rabies and go mad during the dog days of summer.

Finally, there are those "days of auld lang syne" that people toast and sing farewell to on the eve of the new year. *Auld lang syne* is Scottish dialect for "old long since," or days gone by. As another year is rung in, we take a last look at the passing year with the many months, weeks, and days into which we divide time.

As Saturn was the god of time, it seems fitting that the Romans named the final day of the week after him. But time, of course, never really ends. So Saturn was given another symbol to carry besides his harvester's sickle. He was sometimes shown holding a serpent biting its own tail.

The serpent was in the shape of a circle. Like a circle it had no beginning and no end; it represented eternity. The tail-biting serpent of the Roman god Saturn is actually time itself, which is made up of nothing more than the procession of the days.

Bibliography

Asimov, Isaac, *The Clock We Live On*. New York: Abelard-Schuman, 1965.

Bettmann, Otto L., *The Good Old Days — They Were Terrible!* New York: Random House, 1974.

Cable, Mary and the Editors of American Heritage, *American Manners and Morals*. New York: American Heritage, 1969.

Chambers, Robert, *The Book of Days*. Detroit: Gale Research Company, 1967. (reprint; first published 1862–1864, London: W. & R. Chambers)

Cotterell, Arthur, *A Dictionary of World Mythology*. New York: Putnam, 1979.

Couzens, Reginald C., *The Stories of the Months and the Days*. Detroit: Gale Research Company, 1970. (facsimile reprint of 1923 edition)

Gregory, Ruth W., *Anniversaries and Holidays*. Chicago: American Library Association, 1975.

Harper, Howard V., *Days and Customs of All Faiths*. New York: Fleet Publishing Corporation, 1957.

Schmidt, Joël, *Larousse Greek and Roman Mythology*. New York: McGraw-Hill, 1980.

Strasser, Susan, *Never Done: A History of American Housework*. New York: Pantheon Books, 1982.

Index